Goldfish and Chrysanthemums

by **Andrea Cheng**

illustrated by **Michelle Chang**

LEE & LOW BOOKS Inc. • New York

Ni Ni (nie-nie): Grandma
Ba Ba (ba-ba): Dad
Suzhou (sue-joe): a city in eastern China

Text copyright © 2003 by Andrea Cheng
Illustrations copyright © 2003 by Michelle Chang

LEE & LOW BOOKS Inc., 95 Madison Avenue, New York, NY 10016
leeandlow.com

Manufactured in China by South China Printing Co., March 2012

Art direction and book design by Aileen Friedman
Book production by The Kids at Our House

The text is set in ITC Tiepolo Bold
The illustrations are rendered in oil paint

HC 10 9 8 7 6 5 4 3 2 1
PB 10 9 8 7 6 5 4 3 2 1
First Edition

Library of Congress Cataloging-in-Publication Data
Cheng, Andrea.
Goldfish and chrysanthemums / by Andrea Cheng ; illustrated by Michelle Chang.— 1st ed.
p. cm.
Summary: A Chinese American girl puts her goldfish into a fish pond that she creates and borders with
chrysanthemums in order to remind her grandmother of the fish pond she had back in China.
ISBN 978-1-58430-057-1 (HC)   ISBN 978-1-60060-889-6 (PB)
[1. Grandmothers—Fiction. 2. Immigrants—Fiction. 3. Fish ponds—Fiction. 4. Chinese Americans—Fiction.
5. Goldfish—Fiction. 6. Fishes—Fiction. 7. Flowers—Fiction] I. Chang, Michelle, ill. II. Title.
PZ7.C41943 Go 2003   [E]—dc21   2002067113

To Ni Ni, with love—A.C.

To my family, with love—M.C.

Grandma Ni Ni was in the kitchen, cutting carrots into flower shapes. I stood next to her, washing the rice. When Ni Ni first came to live with us, she showed me how to pour cold water on the rice, swirl the rice around with my hand, and pour off the extra water.

Ni Ni smiled. "You are a very good cook, Nancy," she said.

At that moment my brother, Greg, came in with the mail. He handed Ni Ni a thin blue envelope.

"From my brother in China," Ni Ni said, opening the envelope carefully so I could have the stamps. Two photographs fell onto the counter. One was of an old house with a courtyard in the middle. In the other only half the house was standing, and workmen were carting away old bricks and wood.

Ni Ni scanned the letter quickly.

"Brother says the city needs space for apartment building, so they tear down our father's old house in Suzhou," Ni Ni said softly. She held the photos to the light from the window. "Ba Ba had a fishpond in the middle," she said, pointing to the courtyard. "All day I follow him, help him pinch the buds and feed the fish."

Ni Ni's voice cracked. She put down the pictures and went back to her carrot flowers. One broke and she turned it into two carrot fish.

We watched Ni Ni for a few moments. Then Greg asked if we could go to the summer fair in the schoolyard with his friend Nathan. Ni Ni nodded and gave us each a few dollars to spend.

At the fair Greg and Nathan ran right to the rides. I wandered around by myself, trying to decide how to spend my money. I wanted to get something to cheer up Ni Ni, but all I saw was plastic jewelry and toys.

I walked on and came to a booth with rows and rows of fishbowls and a sign that said WIN A GOLDFISH! I decided to try and win one for Ni Ni. When it was my turn, I took a ball and aimed carefully for the back corner. The ball landed in a bowl and I won a fish. I threw again and won a second time. The lady at the booth congratulated me and gave me a bowl with two fish.

When it was time to leave, I followed Greg and Nathan down the street, walking slowly so the water wouldn't slosh out of the goldfish bowl.

At home Ni Ni was upstairs writing a letter. The paper was filled with Chinese characters.

"I won two goldfish," I said, showing Ni Ni the bowl. "Were your Ba Ba's fish like these?"

"Very pretty," Ni Ni said, looking at the fish swimming back and forth. "Ba Ba's the same, only bigger. And all around the pond, big flowers. Yellow ones. Don't know the name in English."

I looked out the window at the yellow and red flowers in our neighbor Mrs. Zalinsky's garden. "Chrysanthemums?" I asked.

Ni Ni looked up. "Maybe," she said. "How do you say . . ."

"Chry-san-the-mums," I repeated slowly.

"Chry-san . . . chry-san . . . the-mums," Ni Ni said. "Garden had a stone path. A bench too. Ba Ba won prizes for his fish and flowers. So beautiful." Then she turned back to her letter.

I went out to the backyard. Underneath our big honeysuckle bush was a puddle where the rain had pooled. Suddenly I had an idea. This would be the perfect place for a fishpond!

I waited and waited for Mom and Dad to come home. When I heard the car, I ran out to meet them.

"Can I dig a fishpond underneath the honeysuckle bush for our new goldfish?" I asked.

"Goldfish? Where did you get goldfish?" Dad asked.

"At the fair in the schoolyard," I said. "I won them, and I want to make a pond for Ni Ni."

Mom looked surprised. "Why?"

"Because her brother said they're tearing down their Ba Ba's house in Suzhou, the one with the pond and garden and everything."

Mom looked at Dad, and he nodded. Then Mom took my hand. "A fishpond is a good idea," she said softly.

The next morning I woke up early. After breakfast I ran to the garage and grabbed the shovel. Then I started to dig under the honeysuckle bush. The top layer of soil was easy to lift but underneath was heavy clay. When I got out most of the clay, I discovered a big root right in the middle of the hole. I pushed the shovel under the root, but no matter how hard I leaned on the handle, I couldn't get it out.

"Quite a project, Nancy," said Mrs. Zalinsky, walking over.
"What are you planting?"

"I'm making a fishpond," I said.

"Looks like you've got a stubborn root there," Mrs. Zalinsky
said. "Maybe I can help." We pushed on the shovel together, and
finally the root came flying out of the ground.

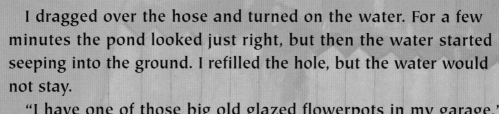

I dragged over the hose and turned on the water. For a few minutes the pond looked just right, but then the water started seeping into the ground. I refilled the hole, but the water would not stay.

"I have one of those big old glazed flowerpots in my garage," Mrs. Zalinsky said. "I think it would be perfect for your pond."

"Are you sure you don't need it?" I asked.

Mrs. Zalinsky said she was sure. We carried the pot to my backyard, and I began to dig the hole deeper. By noon the pot fit perfectly. Then came the test. I filled the pot with water and counted to one hundred. The water was still there.

I cleared away some of the dirt and then went inside to wash my hands. "What you do out there so long, Nancy?" Ni Ni asked.

I tried not to smile. "Just playing," I said, and I ran back outside.

"Hey, Nancy, what are you doing?" Greg asked. He'd been playing ball all morning and had just gotten home.

"Testing my goldfish pond," I said.

"Are you really going to put your fish in it?"

"Remember Ni Ni told us about her Ba Ba's fishpond in Suzhou?" I said. "I'm making a fishpond here, for Ni Ni. Do you want to help me fix it up?"

"Sure," Greg replied.

After lunch we hunted for stones to make the path. Greg
pulled out the old picnic bench from the garage and put it
next to the pond. We heard the backdoor open, and Ni Ni
headed out to see what we were doing.

"Don't look, Ni Ni," I shouted. "It's a surprise."

"I cover my eyes. Don't see anything," Ni Ni said, putting
her hands over her eyes and heading back into the house.

I remembered the chrysanthemums in Mrs. Zalinsky's garden. I ran next door and asked if she had any extras.

"Help yourself," she said. "Just dig them up from the back. They spread there every year."

I thanked Mrs. Zalinsky. Then Greg and I dug up a few clumps, careful to get all the roots, and we planted them around the pond.

"I think it's time for the fish," Greg said.

I went around the front of the house so Ni Ni wouldn't see me get the fishbowl. I carried it carefully to the pond. At the count of three I poured the fish gently into their new home. At first they were stunned, but after a few seconds the fish began swimming every which way.

Ni Ni was in the kitchen, slicing green onions into slivers.

"The surprise is ready," I said. "Close your eyes."

Ni Ni dried her hands, and Greg and I led her to the backyard.

"Now you can open your eyes."

Ni Ni blinked for a minute in the bright sun. Then she smiled.

"So beautiful," she said, squeezing our hands. "So very beautiful."
She saw the flowers and bent down to smell the leaves.

"What did we call them?" Ni Ni asked. Then it came to her.
"Chry-san . . . chry-san-the-mums!" she exclaimed, and we could
see tears in her eyes. We watched the fish for a long time.

s at the Pond

the fish Pond

"We can take pictures!" Ni Ni finally said. "Send to my brother in China. Cheer him up. He can see here we have new pond, baby goldfish, and flowers. We call it Ba Ba's Garden in America."

Greg went to get the camera. Mrs. Zalinsky took a picture of the three of us on the bench with the pond in front. I took a picture of Ni Ni smelling the chrysanthemum leaves.

When Mom and Dad came home from work, Ni Ni told them all about the new garden. "Has two baby goldfish," she said, smiling. "After dinner we can see."

Ni Ni had made six different dishes for dinner. Everything looked so pretty, especially the asparagus with carrot flowers. Then I saw a carrot fish had landed in my bowl. Greg found one too. I looked up at Ni Ni and I knew she had placed them there especially for us.